NAMES LIKE PRAYERS

Names Like Prayers

First Edition

Edited by Georgia Austin

Cover design by Jeffrey Kosh Graphics

ISBNs

Print: 979-8-89934-009-3

ePub: 979-8-89934-008-6

NAMES LIKE PRAYERS

A Novel for Readers Who Refuse to Look Away

GENE SCOTT

CHAPTER ONE

Desmond – The Hunter's Lie

The nightmare always starts the same way.

Security footage. Timestamp: 14:32:07.

Marcus Thompson, seventeen, sits in the Black Hollow common room. Knees bouncing. Hands pressed to his ears like he's trying to keep his skull from splitting open.

"Please," he whispers to the camera. "The voices are getting loud again. Can somebody bring my pills?"

I'm watching through the monitor.

I see him. I hear him.

I don't move.

Legs, stone. Voice, static.

I watch Morrison step forward with the blessed blade.

Marcus rocks like a metronome on a countdown. Still whispering when the steel goes in.

"Des."

Malik's voice cuts through my earpiece. Three years dead, still hunting with me.

"Wake up, brother. You got work."

I wake choking.

Sheets soaked. Room cold. Smells like industrial bleach and sweat.

The hotel clock reads 3:47 a.m.

The hour when memory won't shut up and justice goes silent.

Malik's recorder blinks red on the nightstand.

Still alive. Still listening.

I grab it. Hit record.

"Day 1,095 since Black Hollow. Testimony in six hours. The dream's worse. Marcus asked for his meds. I couldn't—"

Voice gone.

Three years of chasing truth, and I still can't help a boy who's already gone.

"You didn't fail him," Malik says through

static. "The system did. You're here to prove it."

I press the recorder to my chest. It hums warm.

Maybe it's just the battery.

Maybe it's more than that.

Then the hotel phone rings.

Four a.m.

Unlisted number. That always means trouble. Or truth. Sometimes both.

"Mr. Rios?"

The voice belongs to Senator Patricia Martinez. Tired. Controlled. Barely.

"We need to meet. Before the hearing."

"What kind of meeting?"

A pause. Just long enough to check for danger.

"The kind that might get you killed. Room 1247. Ten minutes."

Click.

I pull on yesterday's clothes, grab the recorder, and take the stairs.

Elevators are for people who aren't on target lists.

The hallway is quiet except for the buzz of cheap lighting and a distant ice machine rattling like it's nervous.

Martinez opens the door before I knock.

She's already pouring coffee.

Behind her, archive boxes line the walls —each one stamped BLACK HOLLOW.

They sit like coffins, pretending to be storage.

She hands me a manila folder.

CLASSIFIED — CONGRESSIONAL EYES ONLY

First photo: Valerie Hendricks and James Murphy, both in correctional uniforms, standing at the facility gate. Clipboard in hand.

Timestamp: three hours before the killings started.

"They were federal witnesses," Martinez says. "Scheduled to testify. They died before they could."

She sets her cup down with both hands, like it weighs more than coffee.

"Valerie had evidence. Guards selling drugs during visitation. Murphy testified about assaults on disabled inmates. They

were transferred three days before the pro-
gram started."

I flip through the file.

Wire transfers into campaign war chests.
Medication logs that show systematic
denial.

Transfer orders signed by the same
people who approved funding.

"This was coordinated," I say. "Not a fail-
ure. A blueprint."

Martinez nods once.

"My son died in county lockup seven
years ago," she says. "They said suicide.
Truth is, he saw a guard beat an old man to
death."

The silence after that feels earned.

"You warning me?"

"Or recruiting me?"

"Both."

Straight face. No blink.

"When you testify, the whole country
will be watching. Say their names, Desmond.
Don't let them bury this again."

I think of Marcus.

Of Malik.

Of the journalist who bled truth until they silenced her for good.

"I've been ready since they killed my brother."

"Good."

She passes me one last page.

Handwriting I know better than my own.

Des—If you're reading this, they got me.

Black Hollow was a test site.

Look at Cookeville, Limestone, Hays.

Same grants. Same behavioral teams. Twelve states.

Don't let them bury this with me. — M

I fold the letter and slide it into my inside pocket. Right next to the recorder.

"How long have you had this?"

"Yesterday. Dr. Volkova's car went into the Potomac. They're calling it an accident. It wasn't."

Martinez moves to the window. Fogged glass. Empty street below.

"This isn't just about one facility. It's a network. Systematic witness elimination, dressed up as behavioral reform. It's state-sanctioned erasure."

"What do you need from me?"

"Everything. Names. Dates. Money trails. Proof that doesn't flinch."

I start to leave. Her voice stops me.

"Valerie Hendricks had a daughter. Lucy. Eight years old. She still thinks her mom's working a double shift."

I close my eyes.

That kind of waiting never heals.

"Tomorrow I'll say Valerie's name. And Marcus's. And every name they tried to delete."

"Even if it ends you?"

I pull out the recorder.

"Only then."

Outside, the sun crawls up.

Inside, I sit with a cup of cooling coffee

and enough evidence to burn down every lie they've built.

"Day 1,095," I say into the recorder. "Senator Martinez lost her son to the same machine that took Malik. She's been working from the inside. I've been digging from the outside."

I can hear traffic start up.

The day making noise like it deserves to.

"Found Malik's final note. Twelve states. Same grants. Same kill switch.

They called it behavioral reform. It was erasure."

A pause. Breath. The room's too quiet.

"Today I speak their names. All of them."

Click.

I pocket the recorder.

Then I get ready to make it loud.

CHAPTER TWO

Mama E – The Body Remembers

The body keeps time.

Not in years or birthdays, but in the way knees ache when storms roll in. In the hitch in your chest when you pass the room where something broke. In how certain names taste like pennies.

Mama E wakes before the light.

Always has.

Prayer doesn't keep time—it starts it.

She lays a hand over her chest.

Still breathing.

Still here.

The cot creaks as she sits up. Her knees whisper: it's going to rain.

Outside the shelter, streetlights flicker like tired eyes refusing to close.

She pulls on a knit shawl, soft with age, and opens the box beneath her cot.

The ledger waits inside.

Red leather. Gold thread. A crack in the spine from too much truth pressed between the pages.

She flips to the last entry.

MARCUS THOMPSON

17. Epilepsy. Voices. Left waiting too long.

The ink is smudged, but the name holds.

She picks up her pen.

VALERIE HENDRICKS

42. Guard. Whistleblower. Mother. Loved jazz and late-night radio. Died trying to do right.

The page drinks the ink. Memory becoming artifact.

A soft chime: her phone, face down beside the cot.

She lifts it.

DESMOND RIOS

Need your voice. They're asking for a state-

ment. Something written. Something real. I'll carry it with me. Only if you want.

She reads it twice.

Then once more.

She looks back at the ledger.

Behind her, the kettle starts to sing.

She moves to the kitchenette and pours water over herbs she dried herself.

Sage. Lemongrass. A little ginger—for clarity.

A knock.

"Come in," she calls. Her voice always had weight. Even in the early hour.

Tariq steps in. Hoodie zipped. Shoulders hunched against the morning cold.

"Didn't mean to wake you."

"You didn't. I been up. Storm's coming. My knees told me."

He offers a small smile. Not the kind you believe. The kind you wear.

"I saw the news. Desmond's testifying."

Mama E nods. She stirs the tea. Hands him a mug without asking.

"He's going to say the names," she says.

"You think they'll listen?"

"They'll hear him. Listening's another matter."

He stands by the window, hands around the mug like he's trying to warm something deeper than fingers.

"They tried to pay me to stay quiet," he says. "Man in a suit. Said he could help with tuition. Called it a 'discretionary grant.'"

Her gaze sharpens.

"What'd you say?"

"I told him my mother raised me better."

Mama E nods.

"That she did."

From the drawer, she pulls a small bundle wrapped in cotton. Tied with twine.

"Here."

He opens it slowly.

A square of faded red cloth.

A single name stitched in black thread:

MALIK RIOS

"I made this after the vigil," she says. "Every time someone passes, I sew. It's not much. But it lasts."

He runs a thumb over the stitches.

"Will you make one for me someday?" he asks.

"Don't make me do that," she says.

Not soft. Not cruel. Just true.

Silence. Full of things not said.

"I've got class," he says. "Midterms."

She nods.

At the door, he turns back.

"Thanks for the tea."

"For the name," she says.

He nods once. Then he's gone.

Mama E lifts the ledger again. The weight of it has changed.

Or maybe she has.

She scrolls to Desmond's message again. Rereads it. Then sets the phone beside the open page.

She draws a fresh sheet of paper from the envelope drawer.

Hands steady. Spine straight.

She writes:

Names are prayers.

And some prayers are meant to be said out loud.

The ones they tried to silence—we carry those.

We say them.

We stitch them into breath.

Only then can we let them rest.

She folds the page. Slips it into an envelope with Desmond's name. Seals it with wax.

Then she whispers:

"Only then."

And begins to sew.

CHAPTER THREE

Tariq – Echoes in the Static

The recorder won't shut up.

It's not even on. No blinking light. No battery. Just humming.

Tariq holds it in both hands like something alive.

He presses every button. Flips it open. Nothing.

Still, it hums.

Mama E once told him memory makes a sound.

"You just have to be quiet long enough to hear it."

He's been quiet.

Three days now.

And it won't stop.

Class is useless.

The professor's talking about civic responsibility. Something about systems and representation.

Behind her, the dorm TV plays muted footage of Desmond Rios walking into the Capitol.

Satchel in one hand.

Face like he's carved from the day before war.

A girl in the back snorts too loud.

Someone else drops a pen and just leaves it there.

No one's listening.

But they're all watching.

On his way back from class, Tariq passes the Student Center bulletin board.

Right in the center: a flyer.

Testimony. 6:00 p.m. Eastern. Live on campus green. Streamed.

Below it, someone's scrawled:

Ask him why Marcus had to die.

He stares at it for a long second.

Then tears it down.

Crumples it into his jacket pocket.
It doesn't make him feel braver.
Just heavier.

Back in his room, he tosses the recorder on the bed.
It lands upright.
Silent for a beat.
Then:
Click.
A voice.
Not his.
"Tariq, you gotta stop thinking you're the only one who heard the screaming."
He freezes.
It's Malik.
But the recorder's empty.
He's checked. Twice.
He didn't believe in ghosts.
But he believed in memory.
And guilt.
And static that says too much.

. . .

Later, crossing the quad, a white SUV pulls up slow beside him.

Campus security. Marked but clean.

Tinted windows.

The driver's got a fresh shave and no badge.

"Mr. Webb?" the man says.

"Depends."

"Mind if we talk?"

"That also depends."

The man laughs like he's practiced it.

"I think your silence is valuable. So does someone higher up. There's some funding available—for students who understand the importance of discretion."

"Translation?"

"Don't speak. Don't testify. Don't post."

Tariq looks at the guy's face. Calm. Like they're discussing a scholarship.

The man leans on the wheel.

"Think about your future. It's a nice one. Don't burn it down."

He holds out a card. No name. Just an email address:

quietmatters@protonmail.com

Then he drives off.

Tariq watches him disappear through the north gate.

Brake lights blinking like a slow threat.

That night, thunder shakes the windows.

Lightning rolls through the blinds like flashbulbs.

He lies on his back, eyes open, breathing shallow.

His fingers start drumming a rhythm he didn't know he remembered.

Click-click-pause. Click-click-click.

It was Malik's.

The one he used on cafeteria tables—bored or waiting or pretending not to be afraid.

The recorder turns itself on.

His voice, this time:

"I'm scared I'll forget the sound of his laugh."

Then Malik's again:

"Then say it out loud."

Tariq sits up like he's been slapped.

He picks up the cloth Mama E gave him.

The thread under his thumb is warm.

He reaches for the recorder. Hits record.

"Day... I don't know.

Mama E said memory makes a sound. This is mine.

Malik Rios was my friend.

He made me laugh during lights-out.

He hid my insulin when I forgot to lock the drawer.

He didn't deserve to be erased.

None of them did."

He stops.

Breathes.

Presses the button again.

"They want me to be quiet. To be good. To graduate.

But I'd rather fail everything than forget what happened.

You don't heal by forgetting.

You heal by naming."

Click.

The hum stops.

Outside, the rain keeps coming.

The next morning, he sends an email.

To: desmond.rios@protonmail.com

Subject: You said you'd carry it.
Attachment: tariq-testimony.wav
Message:
Say my name too.
Only then.

CHAPTER FOUR

Desmond – The Grief Loop

The room smells like bleach and old coffee.

Desmond sits on a folding chair in the Capitol's prep room. Elbows on knees. Tie loosened.

The room is windowless. Fluorescents hum above.

The clock ticks like a dare.

A man from legal hands him a water bottle. Doesn't ask if Desmond's ready.

That ship sailed.

The folder in Desmond's lap is stamped:

Rios, Malik — Exhibit D

Inside: his brother's chart.

The timeline.

Grainy security stills.

The transcript of a call no one answered in time.

He's read it thirteen times.

Every time, he finds something new to hate.

A door creaks open.

Valerie Hendricks's replacement—a younger woman, all steel and mascara—leans in.

"Fifteen minutes."

Desmond nods. She closes the door.

He stares at the folder again.

The grief loop starts.

Malik, mid-laugh, in the passenger seat.

Malik with peanut butter on his chin.

Malik curled on the shelter floor, voice hoarse.

Malik zipped into a bag.

His phone buzzes.

It's an audio file.

From Tariq.

Desmond hesitates.

Then plays it.

"Malik Rios was my friend..."

He listens.

All of it.

Doesn't breathe much through it.

At the end:

"Say my name too. Only then."

Desmond presses the phone to his chest.

Not long. Just long enough.

Five minutes later, he's led through security.

Hallways buzz with camera crews and clipped heels.

In the hearing room, it's standing room only.

Mama E is there.

Tariq too.

Senator Holt in his stiff suit.

Governor Volkova, remote in her controlled fury.

The families sit close—clustered and braced.

Desmond takes his seat.

The mic is too low. He adjusts it.

Papers shake in his hand. He doesn't care who sees.

Someone from the committee clears their throat.

"Mr. Rios, you may begin."

Desmond lifts his eyes.

"I'm not here to prove anything," he says. "I'm here to name."

He doesn't read the pages.

He doesn't need them.

He names them.

Marcus Thompson.

Valerie Hendricks.

Malik Rios.

Daniel K.

Anita Sosa.

Cameron McGill.

He says their ages.

How they died.

Who watched.

Who didn't.

A murmur stirs.

Someone sobs, sharp and quiet.

Then—

Static.

In his earpiece.

He freezes. Adjusts the wire. No use.

The hum gets louder.

It's the same hum from Malik's recorder.

Then a voice—only in his ear:

"You left me too long."

His chest tightens.

The room is waiting.

Desmond swallows.

Looks at the committee.

Then at the crowd.

Then: he makes a choice.

"There's more."

Gasps. A chair squeaks.

The legal rep blanches.

Desmond lifts a small recorder. Hits play.

"They want me to be quiet. To be good. To graduate.

But I'd rather fail everything than forget what happened..."

It's Tariq's voice, echoing now across the room.

Across the record.

Senator Holt leans forward.

"This wasn't submitted."

Desmond looks him in the eye.

"Neither was Malik."

After the hearing, in the parking garage, a man falls in step beside him.

Too clean. Too polite.

"Mr. Rios."

Desmond keeps walking.

"Strong testimony. Emotional. Risky."

Desmond doesn't stop.

"Let's talk about what comes next," the man says.

"I'm already talking," Desmond says. "You just don't like what I'm saying."

The man puts a hand on Desmond's arm.

Bad idea.

Desmond jerks away.

"Touch me again," he says, "and you'll need more than damage control."

The man's eyes harden.

"Your brother started a fire. Don't fan it too far."

Desmond's face doesn't change.

He walks.

His hands shake once he's behind the wheel.

But he doesn't cry.

Not yet.

At a red light, he pulls a folded note from his pocket.

Names are prayers.

And some prayers are meant to be said out loud.

Mama E's handwriting.

The light turns green.

He drives.

CHAPTER FIVE

Hour Eighteen

The smell hits you first—disinfectant mixed with fear sweat and metal in the mouth, like a punch that hasn't landed yet. But underneath, something else. Something that smells like hope made from notebook paper and stolen moments.

I sit cross-legged on concrete floors, teaching Ashley Porter how to say *hermana* without the hatred her people trained into her voice. Seventeen years old, Aryan Nations tattoo still fresh on her neck, but her eyes carry something softer now—the look of someone learning that love might be stronger than the lies they fed her since childhood.

"*Her-ma-na*," Ashley repeats, the Spanish rolling awkwardly off her tongue. Around us, twelve kids from six different gangs share textbooks made from toilet paper and hope, creating family from the enemies the system told them they were born to be.

"It means sister," I tell her, watching comprehension bloom across her face like sunrise through bulletproof glass. "Not blood sister. Chosen sister."

Luis Delgado looks up from where he's teaching Robert Kim—sixty-seven, Aryan Nations, Parkinson's disease—how to write his granddaughter's name in careful block letters. An MS-13 kid helping an elderly Nazi grandfather remember love across lines carved in blood and blessed by chaplains who turned prayer into policy.

"*Familia*, right?" Luis says, grinning with teeth that remember hunger but have learned to share food anyway. "*Familia* ain't about blood. It's about choice."

I catch his eye and tap my chest twice—our signal. He nods, understanding.

"Ashley, when I say *hermana* in the common room, it means stay close. When

Luis says *mijo,* it means danger from the left. *Abuela* means guards coming."

Ashley's eyes sharpen. "You're making a language they don't understand."

"We're making a language they can't take away." I pull out the paper where I've been mapping our code. "Spanish sounds like gang talk to them. They expect it from MS-13. But we're using it to coordinate."

DeShawn leans in from his corner. "What's my word?"

"*Corazón,*" I tell him. "Heart. When you say it, it means you're sharing medicine."

"And when the time comes?" Robert Kim asks, his voice stronger than his shaking hands. "When they want us to fight?"

"*Somos familia,*" I whisper. "We are family. When you hear that, we all refuse together. No matter what."

This is our sanctuary. Forty-eight square feet of concrete and contraband textbooks, where children who should be killing each other instead choose to save each other's souls. Where Spanish lessons become declarations of war against systems that profit from hate. Where love grows in laboratory conditions specifically designed to eliminate it.

The intercom crackles to life above us. Governor Holt's voice fills the room like smoke from burning bridges:

"Hour eighteen. Divine providence reveals itself through natural selection. Let the strong protect the weak, and let the weak learn strength through tribulation."

Ashley's hand finds mine—Aryan Nations and MS-13, choosing contact across enemy lines while their government calls systematic murder mathematics.

"Maria," she whispers, and for the first time her voice doesn't carry the careful hatred they taught her at twelve, when her stepfather first put his hands where they didn't belong. "What if we don't kill each other? What if we just . . . don't?"

"Then we prove them wrong about irredeemability."

"Even if it gets us killed?"

"*Especialmente* then."

DeShawn Williams sits in the corner, rationing insulin like communion wine, calculating how many doses he can share before his own body fails. Type 1 diabetic, Crip, beautiful in the way that breaks your heart because he's still soft around the edges despite everything the system did to harden him.

"DeShawn," I call softly. "How you holding up?"

He shows me the insulin pen—half empty, maybe six doses left. In a normal world, that's three days of life. In Black Hollow, that's six chances to choose who lives and who dies.

"Thinking about giving Robert my next dose," he says, nodding toward the elderly Nazi who's learned to call Luis *mijo*—my son —while learning to write love letters to a granddaughter who thinks he's already dead.

"DeShawn, that could kill you."

"Maybe. But keeping it could kill him." DeShawn's smile carries three years of Sunday school before his mama died and the streets taught him that stealing medicine was easier than begging for help. "Somebody's got to choose mercy over math."

"*Corazón,*" Luis says quietly, testing the

word. "That's what you're doing. Giving your *corazón*."

Ashley looks between us—two enemies becoming family while their government counts down the hours until systematic elimination begins in earnest.

"Y'all are crazy," she says, but her voice carries wonder instead of judgment. "They gave us weapons and y'all talking about sharing medicine."

"That's how revolutions start, *hermana*. One choice at a time."

The library door cracks open. Sarah McKenzie slips inside—nineteen, Nashville, Aryan Nations, molested at twelve and radicalized by abandonment. But the rage in her eyes has transformed into something protective, fierce love instead of weaponized pain.

"*Abuela*," she says, using our code. "Morrison and his boys. Common room in ten minutes for what they're calling 'final selection.'"

My stomach drops. Final selection. The moment when blessed weapons meet children's hands and systematic elimination becomes statistical reality.

"Sarah, you don't have to—"

"I ain't leaving y'all." She sits beside Ashley, two white supremacists who found sisters in Latina and Black kids because somebody taught them family was stronger than ideology. "Whatever happens, we face it together."

"Remember the words," I tell them quickly. "Remember what they mean. When I say *somos familia,* that's the signal. Nobody picks up weapons. Nobody fights. We stand together."

Luis stands and helps Robert to his feet, steady hands supporting a man whose own people abandoned him to die alone.

"Robert, you don't gotta fight. You don't gotta choose sides. You just gotta remember your granddaughter's name."

"Elena," Robert whispers, Parkinson's making his voice shake but love making it strong. "Her name is Elena, and she's eight years old, and she draws pictures of horses."

"Then that's who you're fighting for. Not for hate. Not for hurt. For Elena who draws horses."

I look around our sanctuary—twelve

children who should be enemies, learning Spanish and sharing insulin and proving that love can grow anywhere if someone's brave enough to plant it.

"Listen," I tell them, my voice carrying the authority of someone who's learned that leadership means choosing death before betrayal. "In five minutes, they're going to try to make us into the monsters our files say we already are. They're going to put weapons in our hands and call it divine judgment."

"What do we do?" Ashley asks.

"We use our words. We stay together. We prove that *familia* is tactical, not just emotional." I reach for the handmade textbook Luis created from stolen paper—*Familia*, written in careful letters across the cover. "And if we die, we die proving them wrong about what children can choose when somebody teaches them they have options."

DeShawn checks his insulin pen one more time.

"How many of us you think gonna make it out?"

"All of us or none of us. That's how family works."

The intercom crackles again. Morrison's voice this time, flat and final:

"All subjects report to common room for final behavioral assessment. Divine providence awaits."

Sarah's hand finds mine. Then Ashley's. Then Luis reaching for Robert, DeShawn connecting the circle—twelve children who built souls from ashes while adults worshipped statistics.

"*Nuestra familia,*" I whisper. Our family.

"*Nuestra familia,*" they echo.

We stand together and walk toward the common room where blessed weapons wait to transform children into statistics. But we don't walk as MS-13 and Aryan Nations and Crips and individual predators marked for elimination.

We walk as siblings who learned Spanish in storage rooms and shared medicine across enemy lines and chose love in laboratory conditions specifically designed to prove love was impossible.

CHAPTER SIX

Mercy in the Margins

The insulin pen weighs nothing in my hands, but it feels heavy as the world.

Two doses left. Maybe three if I water it down, but that's just buying time with borrowed blood sugar. My body's been eating itself since yesterday—muscle turned to glucose, hope turned to ketones, life measured in units of medicine they took away when I needed it most.

Type 1 diabetic since I was seven. Crip since I was twelve, when Mama died and the streets taught me that stealing insulin was easier than begging doctors who looked at my address and decided some children don't deserve healing.

But sitting here in our makeshift sanctuary, watching Robert Kim try to write his granddaughter's name with hands that shake from Parkinson's and love, I'm thinking about different kinds of mathematics.

The kind where one person's death becomes another person's life.

The kind where mercy defeats arithmetic.

"DeShawn," Maria calls softly from where she's teaching Ashley how to say *te amo* without the hatred her stepfather trained into her voice. "How you feeling?"

I check my blood sugar with the contraband glucose meter Luis smuggled from the medical bay. 380. Normal is 100. At 400, I start thinking in minutes instead of hours.

"I'm good," I lie, because family doesn't need to carry each other's dying when they got their own survival to worry about.

But Robert looks up from his letter writing, eyes slower than most but smart enough to recognize the math of medical crisis.

"Boy," he says, his voice slurred by stroke damage but clear with intention, "how much you got left?"

I could lie again. Should lie. Keep the medicine and live another day while an elderly Nazi dies from diabetic ketoacidosis because his own people abandoned him to systematic elimination.

Instead, I show him the insulin pen. Two doses, maybe three.

"Enough for one of us."

Robert's hands stop shaking for just a moment. In that stillness, I see something I never expected from a man with swastika tattoos and a lifetime of weaponized hatred.

I see love. Clean and simple and completely devoid of arithmetic.

"Give it to your friends," he whispers. "That Maria girl, she's—"

"She's not diabetic." I sit beside his wheelchair, close enough to smell the fear sweat and disinfectant that clings to everyone in this place. "You are."

"I'm old. I'm—"

"You're Elena's grandfather."

His breath catches. Elena—eight years old, draws pictures of horses, still thinks her grandfather is a hero instead of a broken man who spent seventy years learning to hate people who looked like me.

"How did you—?"

"Luis told me. Said you carry her picture next to your heart." I reach for the letter he's been writing, see Elena's name written in careful block letters across paper made from torn sheets and contraband pencils. "Said you been learning to love people your ideology told you to hate."

"I don't deserve—"

"Robert, ain't about deserving. It's about choosing."

I look at the insulin pen again, studying it closer. Something catches my eye—the measurement window. I've been rationing so carefully, watering doses down, that I haven't done the actual math in hours.

Two full doses left. Plus what I already diluted in the spare vial Luis found.

My hands shake as I calculate: half dose for me this morning. Quarter dose two hours ago. Robert's been without for eighteen hours, needs a full dose to stabilize. I need . . .

The math stops my breath.

"What is it?" Robert asks.

"The numbers," I whisper. "They work out perfect."

I show him the pen, the spare vial, my calculations on torn paper. "Look—if I take a quarter dose now, you take three-quarters. Then in six hours, we split what's left. With what I already diluted . . ." I do the math again, not believing it. "We both make it to hour thirty-six. Both of us."

"That's impossible," Maria says, looking over my shoulder. "You said there wasn't enough—"

"I was calculating for full doses. For perfect blood sugar. For the mathematics they taught me in the hospital." My voice cracks with something between laughter and tears. "But if we share it different—if we both accept being sick but alive instead of one perfect and one dead—the math works."

Luis leans in, studying my numbers. "You're saying you both survive?"

"I'm saying the mathematics of mercy are different than the mathematics of medicine." I look at Robert, whose eyes are filling with tears. "We both get sick. We both get weak. But we both live long enough for whatever comes next."

"DeShawn," Robert's voice breaks completely. "I can't take your medicine."

"You're not taking it. We're sharing it. Like family."

I pull out the folded paper I've been carrying since hour six—my own letter home, written on toilet paper with stolen ink. Words for my sister Keisha that I'll never get to send but need to say anyway.

Letter Found Later

Found in DeShawn Williams's cell, written on toilet paper with contraband ink. Never sent.

Keisha—

They took my insulin and called it contraband. Probably gonna die in here, but not the way they planned. Found some family among the enemies. White boy named Luis who calls me brother. Old Nazi who's learning to love his granddaughter more than he hates my skin color.

Mama always said diabetes was just a body that couldn't process sweetness right. Maybe

America got the same disease. Too much anger, not enough insulin. System can't break down all the bitterness, so it just stays in the blood until everything starts shutting down.

But here's the thing—I met this old man who's been poisoned by hate for seventy years, and one picture of a little girl drawing horses was all the medicine he needed to start healing.

Maybe love is insulin for the soul.

Tell Elena her grandfather died trying to remember how to be good.

Tell her he learned it from a Crip kid who shared his medicine with his enemy.

—Your brother who chose mercy

"Robert," I say, folding the letter and pressing it into his shaking hands. "I need you to do something for me."

"No." Maria's voice cuts sharp from across the sanctuary. "DeShawn, no. We can find another way."

"There ain't another way, *hermana*."

"There's always—"

"Maria." I meet her eyes, feeling the first wave of lightheadedness wash over me like warm water. "This is the way."

I draw up the doses with hands that remember Mama teaching me this same motion when I was seven, when she was still alive to show me that medicine was love made visible. Three-quarters for Robert. One-quarter for me. Tomorrow we'll split what remains.

"This is impossible," Ashley whispers. "The math shouldn't work."

"Maybe math works different when you're not trying to subtract people," I say, watching Robert inject the insulin. "Maybe when you multiply instead of divide, there's always enough."

He told me once what insulin tastes like when it hits the back of your throat—metallic and sweet, like pennies soaked in syrup, like mercy mixed with iron.

"It tastes like life," he said, and I wondered if communion wine tastes the same to believers: bitter salvation sweetened by necessity.

As I inject my quarter dose, I taste it too —that metallic sweetness of shared survival.

Hour Twenty-Two: The Final Calculation

The common room fills with children holding blessed weapons they refuse to use. Morrison stands at the altar of systematic elimination, Bible open to Psalms that were written to celebrate life, not justify death.

But twelve kids hold hands instead of knives, choosing family over fear while their government calculates profits from their corpses.

My blood sugar reads 290—higher than healthy, lower than deadly. Beside me, Robert's color is already improving, his hands steadier as he grips mine.

"DeShawn," Ashley whispers, like she's seeing a miracle she didn't ask for. "You okay?"

"We're both okay," I tell her, feeling Robert's pulse under my fingers—steady, strong, still here. "We're both gonna make it."

Maria's hand finds mine. Then Luis. Then Sarah. Twelve children who found their souls in hell while adults turned murder into mathematics, holding each other through the final calculation of divine providence.

My body aches from the uneven insulin levels, vision blurry at the edges but not dark. Beside me, Robert breathes steady—not perfect, but alive. The mathematics worked. Not the mathematics of perfect blood sugar or optimal doses, but the mathematics of choosing shared sickness over solitary health.

"Nuestra familia," Maria whispers.

"Nuestra familia," we echo.

And even as my body struggles with the imperfect dose, even as Robert's does the same, even as systematic elimination transforms into systematic love—

I know Elena will grow up with a grandfather who learned that even seventy years of poison can be flushed out by shared medicine.

That mercy has its own mathematics, more precise than any government equation.

That family isn't about blood—it's about blood sugar shared equally when there's just enough for everyone to survive imperfectly together.

Hour Twenty-Four

They'll find us later, Robert and me, both alive against every medical prediction. They'll check their math, run the numbers, try to understand how two doses became enough for two people across eighteen hours.

They won't understand that love multiplies what fear divides.

That mercy has its own insulin, measured in choices instead of units.

That when you stop subtracting people from the equation, the math always works out.

Elena will draw pictures of horses.

Robert will remember how to love.

And somewhere in heaven, Mama will know her boy discovered that sharing medicine doesn't divide it—it multiplies it by the number of people willing to be sick together rather than let one die alone.

Know that familia isn't about blood —it's about sharing whatever keeps you alive.

And I chose to share.

Even when mercy meant imperfect survival.

Most of all then.

CHAPTER SEVEN

The Last Entry in the Lab Notebook

Twelve video monitors line the wall like windows into hell, each screen broadcasting systematic elimination in real time while I reduce human courage to clinical observations.

Monitor 7 catches my attention. Subject 112—Maria Santos, seventeen, MS-13, five foot two with knife scars mapping a childhood stolen by violence—throws herself between attackers and Subject 203: Robert Kim, sixty-seven, Aryan Nations, wheelchair-bound since his stroke.

Four against one. Blessed knives emerge like prayers answered by policy.

I whisper into the comm, breaking protocol: "Run, Maria, run."

Not *Subject 112*. *Maria*.

The moment I use her name instead of her number, I realize I've crossed a line that no amount of academic objectivity can uncross.

Dr. Sarah Chen sits beside me in the observation booth, clipboard balanced on her knee, pen poised to document systematic murder disguised as behavioral research. Behind us, Governor Holt's voice crackles through the intercom system:

"Divine providence works through earthly agents, Doctor. Document what you observe."

But what I'm observing isn't behavioral modification. It's children choosing love over hate in laboratory conditions specifically designed to prove love was impossible.

"Dr. Volkova," Chen says without looking up from her notes, "you're not recording Subject 112's aggressive response to stimuli."

"Subject 112 is protecting an elderly man whose own people left him to die."

"Document the violence, not the motivation."

"The motivation is the data."

Chen's pen stops moving. For three years, we've worked together reducing human suffering to publishable research, turning children's deaths into academic credentials. But today, watching Maria Santos bleed to save someone she should want dead, I can't pretend this is science anymore.

"Anna, remember why we're here."

"To document behavioral patterns in high-stress environments."

"To prove irredeemability. To provide academic justification for enhanced containment protocols." Chen's voice drops to barely above a whisper. "To justify Holt's expansion plan. You know that."

On Monitor 7, Maria falls to her knees beside Robert's wheelchair, blood pooling under both of them like unwanted baptism. More subjects arrive—DeShawn Williams, Ashley Porter, Luis Delgado. Traditional enemies forming a protective circle around a disabled Nazi grandfather.

My hands shake as I write: *Subject 112 displays remarkable moral courage under extreme duress.*

Should have written: *Subject demonstrates aggressive protective behavior requiring enhanced intervention.*

But I can't reduce courage to pathology. Can't turn sacrifice into statistics.

"Dr. Volkova," Governor Holt's voice fills the observation booth like smoke from burning evidence, "are you documenting systematic behavioral breakdown or individual anomalies?"

"Governor, I'm documenting children who are choosing mercy over violence."

"You're documenting subjects who require enhanced containment due to unpredictable behavioral variance."

"No. I'm documenting proof that rehabilitation works when it's actually attempted."

The silence that follows feels like the moment between lightning and thunder. Through the monitors, I watch twelve children hold hands instead of weapons, creating family from enemies while their government calculates profits from their elimination.

Chen sets down her pen. "Anna, changing your reports won't save them."

"But I can stop providing academic cover for genocide."

"This isn't genocide. It's behavioral research."

"Look at Monitor 7. What do you see?"

Chen studies the screen where Maria Santos bleeds out while whispering something to Robert Kim—words of comfort in Spanish, teaching an elderly Nazi grandfather about mercy while dying to protect him.

"I see Subject 112 exhibiting unpredictable protective behavior toward Subject 203."

But then her voice catches. Her pen freezes mid-notation. On Monitor 3, a new subject enters the frame—Subject 84, male, fifteen, Latino, gang tattoos barely healed.

Chen's clipboard slips. Papers scatter across the floor.

"No," she whispers. "No, that's not—"

"Sarah?"

She's standing now, palms pressed against Monitor 3. The boy on screen turns, and I see Chen's face crumble like paper in fire.

"That's Mateo Rivera. I treated him at the free clinic two years ago. Broken arm from his mother's boyfriend." Her clinical distance shatters completely. "He brought me a drawing of a butterfly as payment because his family couldn't afford—"

She stops. Watches Mateo pick up a blessed weapon with hands that once drew butterflies. On Monitor 7, Maria Santos takes her last breath protecting Robert Kim, and on Monitor 3, Mateo Rivera becomes another subject number in Chen's careful documentation.

"I treated that child." Her voice sounds like something breaking underwater. "I set his bone. I told him he was brave. I promised him—"

She grabs her notebook, flips back through pages of clinical observations. Finds Mateo's entry: *Subject 84 displays heightened aggression requiring intervention.*

"I wrote that. About a child who drew me butterflies."

Chen sinks back into her chair, hands shaking as she retrieves her scattered papers. For a moment, I think she might join me in refusing to continue. But then she picks up her pen, straightens her clipboard, and writes with renewed precision: *Subject 84 eliminated at 14:32. Behavioral modification successful.*

"Sarah—"

"I can't save him by refusing to document it." Her voice has gone flat, professional, dead. "At least my notes will be accurate for the historical record."

"You recognize that child."

"I recognize that my mortgage is due. That my daughter needs college tuition. That refusing to document this won't bring back his butterfly drawings." She continues writing without looking at the monitors. "I recognize that some of us can afford conscience and some of us can't."

"Sarah, when did we stop seeing people and start seeing data points?"

"When people started paying us to provide statistical justification for policy decisions."

"When we became complicit in systematic murder."

Chen closes her notebook and removes her wire-rimmed glasses, cleaning them with the careful precision of someone buying time to think.

"Anna, if you file reports claiming these subjects are rehabilitatable, Governor Holt will alter your conclusions anyway. He's done it before."

"Then I'll make my real findings public."

"And destroy your career? Lose your funding? Spend the rest of your life teaching freshman psychology at community colleges?" Chen replaces her glasses and opens her notebook. "For children who are already dead?"

"For children who died proving love is stronger than hate."

On Monitor 7, Maria Santos breathes her last breath while holding Robert Kim's hand —her mouth moving in silent Spanish, lips still forming prayers no microphone could pick up.

I press the emergency stop button. Red lights flash throughout the facility. Guards halt their systematic elimination protocols. For just a moment, the killing stops.

MS-13 and Aryan Nations, choosing contact across enemy lines while their government calls systematic murder mathematics.

"Dr. Volkova," Holt's voice carries new authority through the intercom, "resume behavioral observation immediately."

"Governor, the subjects are demonstrating capacity for moral development under proper therapeutic intervention. I'm recommending immediate cessation of enhanced protocols."

"Doctor, you're documenting systematic behavioral breakdown requiring enhanced containment."

"I'm documenting systematic love requiring enhanced protection."

"Resume observation, Doctor. That's an order."

I look around the observation booth—

monitors showing children dying for choosing mercy, clipboards full of lies dressed as research, cameras recording systematic murder for academic posterity.

"No."

The word hangs in the air like a prayer finally answered.

"Dr. Volkova," Chen whispers, "you can't stop this by refusing to document it."

"Maybe not. But I can stop participating in it."

I remove my ID badge and set it on the table beside my falsified research notes. Three years of reducing human suffering to publishable conclusions, providing scholarly legitimacy for state-sanctioned elimination.

"Sarah, I've spent my career turning children into statistics while calling it behavioral science. Today they're teaching me that love doesn't need documentation—it just needs witnessing."

"Anna—"

"Maria Santos isn't Subject 112. She's a seventeen-year-old who died proving that family is stronger than ideology." I gesture toward Monitor 7, where guards remove Maria's body while Robert Kim cries for the granddaughter who saved his soul. "DeShawn Williams isn't Subject 98. He's a diabetic who shared his insulin with his enemy because somebody had to choose mercy over arithmetic." I pause, feeling the weight of what I missed. "He chose mercy at a molecular level—surrendered his body so someone else could heal. And I called it data."

"And you think emotional language changes the data?"

"I think emotional truth *is* the data."

Chen picks up her pen again and scribbles something quietly. Doesn't look at me.

"Anna, what will you do now?"

Later, I'll read the line she wrote: *Dr. Anna Volkova removed from project due to emotional compromise affecting observational objectivity.*

"Tell the truth about what we documented. Testify that Black Hollow wasn't behavioral research—it was systematic elimination with academic credentials." I watch Monitor 7 go dark as guards disconnect the cameras. "Make sure Maria Santos and De-Shawn Williams and all the rest are remembered as children who chose love, not subjects who required elimination."

"Even if it costs you everything?"

I think about Maria bleeding to protect Robert Kim. About twelve children holding hands instead of weapons. About love growing in laboratory conditions specifically designed to prove love was impossible.

"Maria chose death over betrayal. I think I can choose truth over tenure."

Hour Twenty-Five. When academic objectivity met human love—and lost.

Outside the observation booth, Black Hollow continues its systematic elimination protocols. Guards distribute blessed weapons. Children die for choosing mercy. The mathematics of genocide disguised as divine judgment.

But inside this room, one academic finally chooses witnessing over documenting.

One scholar finally admits that some truths can't be reduced to statistical significance.

One researcher finally understands that

love doesn't need peer review—it just needs someone brave enough to call it by name.

Final research note: *Love is stronger than hate.*

No further documentation required.

CHAPTER EIGHT

Her Name Was Patricia

The federal protection detail sleeps in shifts outside my door.

Inside: fluorescent bathroom light leaking under the door, digits on the bedside clock changing from 3:17 to 3:18, mechanical hum of air conditioning that never stops.

I sit at the small desk by the window. No lights on. City glow through half-closed blinds makes bars across my hands.

The ledger open. Page 221.

My finger traces the last entry. *Tommy Morrison. Age 14. Gadsden, Alabama.* First to die. Never raised a hand.

I turn the page. Blank paper.

The pen weighs nothing. Weighs everything.

I set it down. Pick it up. Set it down.

Outside: siren growing distant. Someone's emergency becoming someone else's memory.

I stand. Walk to the bathroom. Run water. Don't drink. Return to the desk.

The pen again.

I write: *Patricia Hen—*

Stop.

The ink bleeds into paper fibers. I watch it spread.

Tear the page out. Fold it once. Twice. Three times. Until it's small enough to hide in my closed fist.

New page.

I write: *Patricia Hendricks. Age 34. Corrections officer. Federal witness. Mother.*

The pen scratches against paper. In the silence, it sounds like digging.

I close the ledger. Both hands flat on the cover. The leather worn soft where my thumbs rest.

Behind me, the clock changes to 3:24.

I open to page one. *Marcus Thompson.*

My finger on his name. Then the next. Then the next.

Some pages stick together—tears dried between them, or coffee spilled during late-night documentation, or just the weight of being opened and closed ten thousand times.

Page 189. I stop.

Ink smudged here. My granddaughter's small handprint in the margin from when Keisha was three, reached for grandmother's work with hands still sticky from peanut butter.

I turn back to the new entry. *Patricia Hendricks.*

Count forward. 222 names now.

The chair creaks when I lean back.

I pull the ledger against my chest. Hold it there. My breathing makes the only sound—in through nose, out through mouth, the way my daughter taught me when the panic attacks started after Black Hollow.

3:31 a.m.

I set the ledger on the desk. Line it up with the edge. Precisely parallel.

Stand. Walk to the window. Part the blinds with two fingers.

Washington, D.C. at night.

Federal buildings lit like tombstones.

Traffic still flowing on Constitution Avenue.

A city that never stops grinding people into policy.

I let the blinds fall closed.

Back at the desk. The torn page still in my fist.

I open my hand. Unfold the paper. *Patricia Hen*— bleeding into creases.

I hold it over the wastebasket.

Hold it.

Hold it.

Set it on the desk beside the ledger.

3:39 a.m.

I open to the last page again.

After *Patricia Hendricks's* name, I draw a line.

Below it, nothing.

Close the ledger.

My hands shake—age or exhaustion or the weight of knowing that tomorrow I speak these names to power and power has weapons blessing themselves in the dark.

I stand. Sit. Stand again.

Go to my purse. Pull out the photo—Keisha at five, missing her front teeth, holding a crayon drawing of 221 stick figures holding hands.

Set it beside the ledger.

3:44 a.m.

I open the hotel room door. The federal marshal in the hallway looks up from his crossword.

I hold up one finger.

Close the door.

Back to the desk. Back to the ledger.

Back to the blank space after the line.

The pen hovers.

I set it down.

Pick up the torn page. Smooth it flat. Fold it again.

Slide it into the ledger at page 17—where DeShawn Williams gave away his last breath.

Close the ledger. *Final.*

3:52 a.m.

I lie on the bed fully clothed. Ledger on my chest. Rising and falling with my breath.

The clock changes to 4:00.

The silence holds everything: every name I spoke. Every name I didn't. Every name still being written in facilities I'll never see.

My breathing slows.

The ledger rises.

Falls.

Rises.

Outside, Washington, D.C. grinds toward dawn and testimony that will change nothing and everything and nothing again.

Inside, silence.

Just silence.

And the weight of 222 names.

Carried by one woman.

Who refuses to let them fall.

CHAPTER NINE

The Trial of America

The courtroom smells like old wood and fresh lies, but underneath it: truth, coiled and waiting to strike. Every seat is packed with families, survivors, reporters, and federal prosecutors who spent six months building an airtight case against systematic witness elimination.

But this isn't just *United States v. William Holt* anymore. This is America asking itself whether genocide becomes acceptable when wrapped in theology and justified by mathematics.

I sit in the gallery beside Desmond and Dr. Volkova, watching Governor Holt represent himself at the defendant's table. He dismissed his legal team two weeks ago, claiming no earthly attorney could defend divine mathematics with the authority it deserves.

"Ladies and gentlemen of the jury," Federal Prosecutor Sarah Chen begins, standing before twelve Americans who will decide whether systematic murder becomes systematic justice when the system orders it, "over the next two weeks, you will hear evidence of the most calculated act of domestic terrorism in modern American history."

She activates a large monitor. Maria Santos's face fills the screen—seventeen years old, smiling in a photo taken three weeks before Black Hollow, back when she believed the system might protect her instead of eliminate her.

"Maria Santos died protecting an elderly Nazi grandfather from attackers who should have been her allies. She chose love over ideology while Governor Holt chose profits over people."

The monitor switches to DeShawn Williams. Nineteen years old, insulin pen in hand, teaching his sister how to calculate proper dosages for diabetic emergencies.

"DeShawn Williams shared his final insulin dose with the same grandfather Maria died protecting. He chose mercy over survival while Governor Holt chose mathematics over medicine."

Twelve faces stare back—working-class Americans confronting systematic murder.

"Members of the jury, the evidence will show that Governor Holt orchestrated the systematic elimination of ninety-three federal witnesses, then provided theological justification for calling it divine judgment."

"Objection, Your Honor," Holt says, rising from the defendant's table with the practiced authority of someone who's never doubted his own righteousness. "Counsel mischaracterizes justified intervention as systematic elimination."

"Sustained," Judge Margaret Torres replies, but her voice carries the weight of someone who's already reviewed six months' worth of evidence. "Mr. Holt, you will limit your objections to matters of law, not theology."

"Your Honor, theology commands law when God speaks through earthly agents."

"Mr. Holt, this is a federal courtroom, not a church. Please be seated."

But Holt remains standing, Bible open in his hands, the same NPR-calm composure that ordered systematic murder three years ago.

"Your Honor, if I may address the jury."

"Mr. Holt, opening statements come after prosecution concludes."

"Then I waive my opening statement in favor of closing argument now." Holt turns to face the jury directly, and I feel the temperature in the room drop ten degrees. "Ladies and gentlemen, examine the results."

He slides a document toward the jury box. Statistical analysis printed on official state letterhead.

"Violence against vulnerable populations: down seventy-three percent since Black Hollow. Sexual assault in correctional facilities: virtually eliminated. Drug trafficking during visitation: reduced ninety-one percent."

The numbers hang in the air like incense at a funeral—ritual smoke hiding the smell of what really died.

"If two hundred twenty-one predators died protecting thousands of innocent lives, isn't that divine mathematics?"

"Objection," Prosecutor Chen says sharply. "Defendant is testifying, not arguing."

"Sustained. Mr. Holt, be seated or I'll hold you in contempt."

"Your Honor, contempt from earthly courts means nothing to agents of divine providence."

That's when I know this trial won't end with justice. It will end with America finally admitting what it's always been: a nation that calls genocide grace when the numbers support the narrative.

Day Three. Survivor Testimony.

Luis Delgado takes the witness stand— twenty-one now, social worker, carries Robert Kim's letter to Elena in his wallet like scripture. Behind him, eleven other

Black Hollow survivors sit in the front row, living witnesses to love triumphing over hate in laboratory conditions.

"Mr. Delgado," Prosecutor Chen begins, "please tell the jury what you witnessed at Black Hollow."

"I saw children choose family over fear. I saw Maria Santos die protecting my grandfather—not blood grandfather, chosen grandfather—because somebody had to prove love is stronger than arithmetic."

"Can you describe the moment weapons were distributed?"

"They blessed the knives with tap water from Poland Spring bottles and called it communion." Luis's voice carries three years of survivor's guilt transformed into witness testimony. "But twelve of us held hands instead of knives."

"Why?"

"Because Maria taught us *familia* isn't about blood—it's about choice."

Holt stands again. "Objection. Witness is providing theological interpretation, not factual testimony."

"Your Honor," Luis says, looking directly at Holt, "you made it theological when you called systematic murder divine judgment."

The gallery erupts. Judge Torres gavels for order, but the damage is done.

Day Seven. The Defendant's Testimony.

"State your name for the record."

"William Jefferson Holt, Governor of Tennessee, earthly agent of divine providence."

If he still had an attorney, they'd be dragging him off the stand by now. But Holt dismissed counsel because he genuinely believes God needs his help separating wheat from chaff through systematic elimination.

"Governor Holt," Prosecutor Chen begins, "did you order the systematic elimination of federal witnesses at Black Hollow?"

"I ordered necessary intervention to protect innocent lives."

"By murdering children?"

"By eliminating future predators."

"Marcus Thompson wanted to be a nurse."

"Marcus Thompson was a drug dealer. Age doesn't change nature."

Chen lets him talk, lets the jury hear every justification, every word that proves systematic witness elimination was policy, not accident.

Day Fourteen. Jury Deliberation.

They're out for eighteen hours. When they return, one juror comes back with eyes red from crying. Another avoids eye contact with the gallery entirely.

"Has the jury reached a verdict?"

"We have, Your Honor."

"On the charge of conspiracy to commit murder, how do you find?"

"We find the defendant . . . guilty."

The courtroom erupts, but it's not celebration. It's the sound of a democracy finally admitting it almost murdered itself through divine mathematics.

"Guilty on all counts—conspiracy, terrorism, racketeering." The words pile up like bodies.

But I watch the jury's faces. This isn't justice—it's sacrifice. They're convicting Holt to protect the system that created him.

After the Verdict. Courthouse Steps.

"Mrs. Washington," a reporter calls as we exit the federal courthouse, "how do you feel about the conviction?"

I think about Marcus Thompson asking for medication that never came. About De-Shawn Williams sharing insulin across enemy lines. About 221 children who proved love is stronger than hate while their government chose mathematics over mercy.

"Baby, they convicted one man to protect a system that creates more like him. Governor Holt wasn't an aberration—he was implementation."

"Are you saying justice wasn't served?"

"I'm saying justice starts with conviction and ends with transformation. We got half the equation."

Desmond approaches, holding Malik's

recorder like evidence of everything the system refuses to admit.

"Mama E's right. Holt goes to prison, but the network he built spans twelve states. The theology he preached is spreading online."

Dr. Volkova joins us, still wearing the hospital bracelet from her 'car accident' six months ago.

"The academic framework that justified Black Hollow is being taught in criminal justice programs across the country. We stopped one architect, but we didn't stop the blueprint."

I look back at the courthouse. Behind those marble columns, America just chose to believe that individual evil explains systematic murder.

Desmond holds up Malik's recorder, still running after all these years. "The investigation continues," he says. "Cookeville, Alabama, Georgia. Same network, new architects."

Dr. Volkova adjusts her hospital bracelet. "Same academic justifications being taught to the next generation of policymakers."

The reporter's microphone catches it all.

"Mrs. Washington, what's next?"

I think about 221 children who chose love over hate in laboratory conditions designed to prove love was impossible. About twelve jurors who chose truth over comfort.

"Next, we keep saying their names. Keep documenting the truth. Keep choosing love over mathematics."

"Even if it changes nothing?"

Always then.

CHAPTER TEN

Mama E—The Eternal Ledger

Six Years After the Verdict – Memphis, Tennessee

My granddaughter's hands are smaller than mine, but they hold the pen with the same careful authority I learned when writing names became prayer and memory became resistance.

"Tell me about Marcus again, Grandmama."

I sit in my kitchen chair—the same one where I first opened my handwritten ledger to federal investigators six years ago—watching eight-year-old Keisha copy names into her own notebook. The original ledger rests open between us, pages yellowed but ink still dark, each name still glowing soft when written with love—not literal light, but the kind that comes when you refuse to let someone's death be reduced to statistics.

"Marcus Thompson, age seventeen. Memphis, Tennessee. Wanted to be a nurse. Helped his grandmother with her insulin shots."

"Why did they kill him, Grandmama?"

"Because he saw guards selling medicine to families who couldn't afford it, and he thought telling the truth would help people."

"Was he wrong?"

I think about the memorial five miles away, where thousands gather each year to speak 221 names. About Marcus Jr. healing diabetic children in his uncle's memory. About DeShawn Thompson-Williams learning Spanish across enemy lines in elementary school classrooms named after eliminated witnesses.

"No, baby. He was just early."

Keisha writes *Marcus Thompson* in careful letters, then looks up with eyes that carry my own stubborn refusal to let systematic elimination become systematic forgetting.

"**Grandmama, will you teach me all their names?**"

"**All 221 of them.**"

"**That's a lot of names.**"

"**That's a lot of children who proved love is stronger than hate.**"

I turn the page to DeShawn Williams's entry, where I'd written: *Shared insulin with enemy because somebody had to choose mercy over mathematics.*

"**But you don't got to carry them all alone.**"

I stand and walk to the kitchen cabinet, removing a cardboard box that's been waiting for this moment since the day congressional testimony transformed individual witness-bearing into collective movement.

Inside: forty-seven handwritten ledgers, identical to mine, copied by families who refused to let 221 names die with one old woman's memory.

"**Baby, look.**"

I show her the ledgers—each one carrying all 221 names, each one distributed to families who lost children, survivors who lived through systematic elimination, and witnesses who chose truth over silence.

"DeShawn Williams's sister keeps one in Birmingham. Maria Santos's mother carries one in Los Angeles. Dr. Volkova teaches from one at the university."

I open another ledger, written in Ashley Porter's careful handwriting: same names, same ages, same stories—but told in the voice of someone who learned Spanish from a dying teenager.

"Every family has one now."
"Why?"
"Because memory shouldn't live in just one place. Because if something happens to me, their names keep getting spoken."

I sit back down and open Keisha's notebook to a fresh page.

"Because the work is bigger than any one person carrying it."
Together we copy Sarah McKenzie's story. *Age nineteen. Nashville. Chose hate because*

love had already failed her, then chose love anyway because somebody had to.

Keisha's pencil moves carefully, forming letters that transform systematic elimination into systematic remembrance.

"Grandmama, how do you know if you're writing their names right?"

"Close your eyes, baby."

She does.

"Picture Sarah McKenzie. Nineteen years old. Hurting from things that happened when she was twelve. Angry because the system taught her that anger was safer than hope."

"I can see her."

"Now picture her teaching Spanish to children who look like the people she was told to hate. Picture her holding hands with Maria Santos while their government called systematic murder divine judgment."

"She's smiling now."

"Open your eyes. Write her name like she's smiling."

Keisha writes *Sarah McKenzie* in letters that seem to glow in the afternoon light streaming through kitchen windows. Not literal light, but the kind that comes when you refuse to let someone's death be reduced to statistics.

"It feels warm when I write it."

"That's love making itself visible, baby. That's what happens when memory becomes prayer."

We continue through the afternoon—name after name, age after age, story after story that transformed individual trauma into collective healing through the simple act of refusing to forget.

As evening approaches, I feel the familiar pull of sleep that's been coming earlier each day. Seventy-eight years of carrying names like prayer beads, six years of congressional testimony and federal trials and systematic retaliation, and my body's ready to rest in the promise that 221 names live in forty-seven ledgers carried by families who'll speak them long after I'm gone.

"Grandmama, you getting tired?"

"A little, baby. But not too tired to teach you one more name."

I turn to the final entry in my original

ledger—a page I wrote three years ago but never showed to congressional investigators or federal prosecutors or anyone else who thought witness-bearing was about justice instead of love.

Evelyn Washington, age 78. Memphis, Tennessee. Kept names when systems tried to erase them. Proved memory is stronger than forgetting.

"Grandmama, that's your name."

"Yes, baby. Because one day, someone's going to need to remember that an old woman chose love over silence, truth over comfort, names over numbers."

"I'll remember."

"I know you will. But more than that—you'll teach other children to remember too."

I close the original ledger and place it in Keisha's small hands.

"This is yours now."

"But Grandmama—"

"The names don't belong to me, baby. They belong to anyone brave enough to speak them."

CHAPTER ELEVEN

Seven Years After Holt's Conviction

Birmingham, Alabama

The warehouse smells like Black Hollow—disinfectant, fear-sweat, and something else I can't name but recognize in my bones. Another "behavioral modification facility." Another systematic elimination site. Another thread in the web Malik died trying to unravel.

I hold his recorder in my hand, still functional after a decade of documentation. The red light blinks in the darkness like a heartbeat that refuses to stop.

"Day 3,652 since Black Hollow," I whisper into the device. **"Malik, I found another one."**

Through the window, I watch guards in corrections uniforms moving through the yard. Same formation as Black Hollow. Same blessed weapons protocols. Same divine mathematics, just with updated language.

They call it the *Restorative Justice Innovation Center* now. The sign out front promises *Evidence-Based Rehabilitation Through Structured Intervention*. But I've tracked seventeen federal witnesses who entered this facility in the last six months.

None of them testified at their scheduled hearings.

My phone buzzes. Text from Keisha Washington—Mama E's granddaughter, now a federal prosecutor with her grandmother's gift for making the dead speak in court.

Patterson case moved to Tuesday. Need your files on the Alabama network.

I text back: **At the Birmingham site now. They're using the same transfer protocols as Black Hollow.**

Three dots appear, then: **How many witnesses?**

Seventeen confirmed. Maybe more.

Get out of there, Des. We need you alive to testify.

But I can't leave. Not yet. Through the window, I see them—a line of new arrivals being processed. Young faces that remind me of Marcus Thompson, of DeShawn Williams, of 221 names that became a litany I can't stop praying.

One boy, maybe sixteen, clutches a photo in his hand. Even from here, I can see his lips moving—talking to the picture like it might answer back. The way I talk to Malik's recorder. The way we talk to our dead when the living won't listen.

A guard approaches him, hand extended for the photo. Standard protocol—no personal items, no connections to the outside world, no reminders that you were human before you became a number.

The boy shakes his head. Holds the photo tighter.

I know how this ends. I've seen it end 221 times before.

"Malik," I whisper into the recorder, **"I can't do this again. Can't document more names without trying to stop it."**

"Des." Malik's voice echoes in my memory—not from the recorder, but from that space where the dead live when we refuse to let them go. **"The work isn't just about documenting. It's about disrupting."**

I pull out my phone and dial a number I memorized but hoped I'd never need to use.

"FBI tip line," the voice answers.

"This is Desmond Rios. I'm a federal witness in the Patterson case. I'm at the Restorative Justice Innovation Center in Birmingham, and I'm watching them process seventeen federal witnesses using Black Hollow protocols."

Silence. Then: **"Mr. Rios, can you maintain visual surveillance without compromising your safety?"**

"For how long?"

"Fifteen minutes. We have units en route."

"Tell them to hurry. They're about to distribute weapons."

Through the window, I watch the boy with the photograph finally surrender it to the guard. But as he does, I see him mouth something to the image. Three words that don't need sound to be understood:

I love you.

The same words Marcus Thompson mouthed to his grandmother's memory. The same words DeShawn Williams wrote to his sister. The same words 221 children spoke to the families they'd never see again.

"Day 3,652," I continue into Malik's recorder. **"Seventeen more names about to join our ledger. But maybe not. Maybe this time, love interrupts the equation before it balances."**

Sirens in the distance. Federal agents arriving to stop another harvest of witnesses. The guards inside beginning to realize something's wrong, beginning to scramble, beginning to understand that someone's been watching.

Someone's been counting.

Someone's been carrying names like ammunition, waiting for the right moment to fire them into the heart of a system that thinks witness elimination is just another form of behavioral modification.

The boy with the photograph looks up at the window where I'm standing. For a moment, our eyes meet across the distance between witness and survivor, between documentation and intervention, between the living and the not-yet-dead.

I hold up Malik's recorder so he can see the red light blinking.

So he knows someone's watching. Someone's recording. Someone's going to make sure his name means more than a number in a system designed to subtract him from existence.

The FBI vehicles screech into the parking lot. Agents pour out with warrants and weapons that don't need blessing because they're aimed at the real predators— the ones who call murder mathematics and dress genocide in bureaucratic language.

"Malik," I say as the agents breach the facility doors, **"we're not just counting the dead anymore. We're multiplying the living."**

Through the window, I watch the boy pick up his photograph from where the guard dropped it in the chaos. He holds it to his chest like Mama E held her ledger. Like I hold this recorder. Like we all hold our dead when we're trying to keep them alive.

The equation is changing.

The mathematics of mercy are finally auditing the mathematics of murder.

And this time, we're going to make sure love shows its work.

Later – Federal Detention Center

Seventeen witnesses sit in protective custody instead of elimination chambers. Seventeen names that won't need to be written in memorial ledgers. Seventeen futures that systematic murder won't get to subtract.

Keisha Washington arrives with a team of federal prosecutors. She carries her grandmother's ledger and the authority to transform memory into indictments.

"Mr. Rios," she says, sitting across from me in the interview room, **"your surveillance just exposed a seven-state network. We're looking at RICO charges against forty-three officials."**

"How many facilities?"

"Twelve confirmed. Same financial structure as Black Hollow. Same private prison funding. Same theological justification." She opens the ledger to a page near the back. **"Same mathematics, different variables."**

I hand her Malik's recorder. Ten years of documentation. Three thousand six hundred fifty-two days of refusing to let the dead stay silent.

"Your brother would be proud," she says.

"My brother would want us to solve the equation, not just document it."

She nods, understanding. **"The equation was never about the math. It was about who gets to decide which lives count."**

Through the window, I can see the boy with the photograph being interviewed by FBI agents. He's showing them the picture —his little sister, maybe eight years old, wearing a school uniform and smiling like she believes the world keeps its promises.

Another Elena drawing horses. Another

reason to keep counting. Another reminder that love multiplies when someone's brave enough to do the math differently.

"What happens now?" I ask.

Keisha closes the ledger and stands. **"Now we prove that systematic witness elimination is a federal conspiracy spanning multiple states. Now we show that Black Hollow wasn't an isolated incident but a beta test for nationwide implementation."**

"And the survivors?"

"They testify. They name names. They transform from victims to witnesses." She pauses at the door. **"They prove that survival is its own form of resistance."**

I pick up Malik's recorder one more time.

"Day 3,652. We interrupted the equation. Seventeen witnesses breathing instead of bleeding. Seventeen names that won't need memorial but will provide testimony."

The red light blinks steady. Still recording. Still carrying voices across the divide between justice and silence.

But now those voices include the living.

Now the equation includes variables like hope.

Now the mathematics of mercy don't just audit death—they multiply life.

Malik's work continues. The documentation evolves into disruption. The counting transforms into accountability.

And somewhere in heaven, 221 children watch us finally learning their lesson:

Love doesn't just survive the equation.

Love changes how we calculate.

Forever.

CHAPTER TWELVE

The Communion of Names

Memphis, Tennessee. 5:47 a.m.

Keisha Washington teaches her daughter Spanish in the kitchen where her grandmother once taught her to write names like prayers. The original ledger sits open between them, a third hand reaching across generations.

"Hermana," six-year-old Amara repeats, the word rolling off her tongue with the same careful attention her great-grandmother gave to each of the 221 names. **"It means sister, but not blood sister. Chosen sister."**

"That's right, baby." Keisha touches the page where Maria Santos's name glows in morning light. **"Maria Santos taught those words to children who were supposed to be her enemies. She proved that family isn't about blood—"**

"It's about choice," Amara finishes, because she's heard this story before. Will hear it again. Will teach it to her own children someday.

The kitchen smells like coffee and memory. On the wall, a photograph: Evelyn Washington holding the ledger, surrounded by the forty-seven families who carry copies now. Below it, a newer photo: Keisha being sworn in as U.S. attorney for the Western District of Tennessee, the ledger on the Bible beneath her hand.

"Mama, why do we have to remember all their names?"

"Because names are prayers, baby. And prayers get answered by people willing to do the work."

Birmingham, Alabama. 6:15 a.m.
DeShawn Williams's sister Latasha opens the free diabetes clinic she founded in

her brother's memory. The waiting room already holds seventeen people who can't afford insulin any other way.

She unlocks the medicine cabinet and counts doses. Always enough, somehow. Not because the math works perfectly, but because when word spread about a clinic that never turns anyone away, donations multiplied like loaves and fishes.

On the wall, DeShawn's letter: *Maybe love is insulin for the soul.*

"Morning, Ms. Williams," Robert Kim Jr. says, entering with a box of supplies. He volunteers here every week, honoring the grandfather who learned too late that medicine shared is medicine multiplied. **"Delivery from the Santos Foundation just arrived."**

Latasha smiles. The Santos Foundation —started by Maria's mother, funded by families who refuse to let their children's deaths be the end of their stories. They ensure no diabetic child dies for lack of insulin. They ensure love remains molecular, practical, measurable in lives saved.

"How many patients today?"

"Thirty-two scheduled. But you know how it is."

She does. They never turn anyone away. The mathematics of mercy don't calculate scarcity—they create abundance through the simple act of sharing what seems insufficient.

Los Angeles, California. 7:30 a.m.

Ashley Porter teaches at Maria Santos Elementary, where every child learns Spanish as a second language and love as a first principle. Her Aryan Nations tattoos have faded to ghostly reminders beneath long sleeves, but her students know her story. Know how Maria Santos taught her that *hermana* was stronger than hatred.

"Somos familia," the children chant during morning assembly, their voices carrying across the playground where municipal officials once wanted to build another juvenile detention center.

Now it's a school. Now it's a garden where children who might have been sorted into gangs learn to sort themselves into study groups. Where love grows in what used to be concrete designed for elimination.

Ashley watches them file into classrooms, these children saved from systematic sorting by adults who learned that divine mathematics could be countered with human addition.

Her phone buzzes. Message from Luis Delgado: **Federal judge just approved the consent decree. All twelve states have to implement our curriculum.**

She smiles. Their curriculum—teaching rehabilitation through relationship, mercy through mathematics, family through choice. What started in a storage room at Black Hollow has become federal education policy.

Transformation through legislation. Memory through policy. Love through law.

Washington, D.C. 9:00 a.m.

Dr. Anna Volkova, now secretary of rehabilitation services, stands before Congress to deliver her annual report. Behind her, screens show data that would have been impossible under the old mathematics:

- Witness intimidation: down 89 percent
- Successful rehabilitation: up 76 percent
- Recidivism: at historic lows
- Federal witnesses surviving to testify: 99.7 percent

"Ladies and gentlemen," she begins, her voice carrying the weight of someone who once documented death and now documents resurrection, **"the evidence is clear. When we invest in rehabilitation instead of elimination, when we choose mercy over mathematics, when we treat children as redeemable rather than disposable . . ."**

She pauses, remembering Maria Santos bleeding out on Monitor 7. Remembering when she finally chose witnessing over documenting.

"We don't just save money. We multiply miracles."

Atlanta, Georgia. 11:00 a.m.

Judge Patricia Martinez presides over

the latest trial of officials who thought witness elimination was just good business practice. In her courtroom, the original ledger has become legal precedent. The 221 names have become 221 reasons why systematic murder is always systematic murder, no matter what language it wears.

"The defendants will rise."

Forty-three corrections officials stand, about to learn that divine mathematics can't protect you when human love does the accounting.

In the gallery, families hold their own ledgers. Not in mourning anymore, but in witness. Not in grief, but in power. They've transformed from victims to victors through the simple act of refusing to let memory remain memorial.

Nashville, Tennessee. 2:00 p.m.

Dale Morrison's son—Morrison Jr., who once thought blessing weapons made murder holy—now serves as chaplain at a rehabilitation center. Real rehabilitation, not elimination disguised as intervention.

He leads a prayer circle where former enemies hold hands. Where Spanish-speaking kids teach English-speaking kids that *familia* doesn't require translation. Where insulin gets shared and mathematics get reimagined and love gets chosen over hate because somebody has to start.

"Father, teach us to multiply mercy," he prays, his voice carrying his father's cadence but not his father's theology. **"Show us how to calculate grace."**

The young people bow their heads, these would-be statistics who became testimonies instead. They pray in different languages but with one voice:

Somos familia.

Memphis, Tennessee. 5:00 p.m.

Keisha Washington stands at her grandmother's grave, the original ledger in one hand, her daughter's hand in the other. The headstone reads simply:

Evelyn Washington

1950–2033

She Kept the Names

But the real memorial is in the forty-seven ledgers carried by forty-seven families. In the Spanish words spoken by children who never met Maria Santos. In the insulin shared by people who learned that medicine multiplies when divided properly. In the federal laws that now protect witnesses instead of eliminating them.

"Tell me about Grandmama again," Amara says.

"She was a woman who turned grief into gravity. Who made memory into justice. Who proved that love is stronger than mathematics."

"Was she right?"

Keisha looks around the cemetery where 221 names have become 221,000 saved lives through systematic change. Where witness elimination has become witness protection. Where divine mathematics has been audited by human love and found forever wanting.

"Yes, baby. She was right."

They walk back through the cemetery as evening falls. Behind them, Evelyn Washington's grave glows in the last light—not literally, but with the kind of radiance that comes when someone's life becomes larger than their death.

At home, Keisha opens the ledger to the last page. After her grandmother's final entry, she writes:

The names continue. The work evolves. Love multiplies.

—Keisha Washington, granddaughter, federal prosecutor, keeper of names

Teaching my daughter what my grandmother taught me:

That memory is ministry.

That justice is generational.

That mercy is mathematics.

That naming the dead teaches the living how to count.

Amara watches her mother write, then picks up her own pen. In careful letters, she adds:

Amara Washington, age 6. Great-granddaughter. Learning to write names like prayers.

Three generations holding one ledger.

Three women refusing to let systematic murder have the last word.

Three keepers of names proving that

love doesn't just survive systems designed to eliminate it.

Love redesigns the system.

Love rewrites the equation.

Love makes the last word first, and the first word eternal:

Familia.

Now and always.

Forever and ever.

Amen.

Keisha closes the ledger, turns to her daughter, and says,

"Now let's teach them how to count the right way."

Somewhere, a new name waits.

Pen in hand..

CHAPTER THIRTEEN

A Reader's Guide for Those Who Refuse to Forget

"Write her name like she's smiling." —*Mama E*

Where to Start: Questions That Change Everything

Some books entertain. Others educate. This one demands you choose what kind of person you'll be after reading it. These questions don't just start conversations—they reveal who you really are when it matters.

• Which character made you most uncomfortable—Desmond's relentless investigation, Mama E's public testimony, Dr. Volkova's academic complicity, or Morrison's weaponized faith? What does your discomfort tell you about yourself?

• When Maria teaches Spanish to children programmed to hate each other, transforming language into tactical resistance, what does this say about education as revolution?

• DeShawn and Robert both survive by sharing insulin imperfectly. What does this mathematical miracle say about abundance versus scarcity thinking?

• Morrison blesses weapons with tap water and calls it holy. How does language in your community make harmful things sound acceptable?

• The trial convicts one man but leaves the system intact. What problems in your community get blamed on "bad individuals" instead of broken systems?

• By the end, children attend Maria Santos Elementary School. How do we move from remembering tragedy to preventing it?

About This Guide

Names Like Prayers asks whether love can survive in institutions engineered to erase compassion. Whether citizens can choose moral courage when systems demand silence. Whether children already know what justice looks like—and we just stopped listening.

Content note: This book depicts systematic violence against children, religious justification for harm, and institutional complicity in elimination policies. It may be difficult for readers who've witnessed how systems fail the people they're meant to protect.

How to use this guide: Choose the sections that speak to your experience. Share the questions that challenge your assumptions. Most importantly, let this story change how you see the systems you encounter every day.

This won't be easy. That's the point. Start where it hurts. Keep going when it matters.

Part I: When Good People Stay Silent
Chapters 1–2: The Weight of Witness
Desmond's Investigation
A brother carrying his dead sibling's

voice, determined to expose the truth—even when truth-telling becomes dangerous. His nightmares of Marcus Thompson asking for medication show how trauma becomes fuel for justice.

Mama E's Testimony

A grandmother transforms her handwritten list into federal evidence, proving that sometimes the most powerful weapon against institutional violence is one person refusing to forget.

For reflection:

• When have you known something was wrong but stayed quiet for safety reasons?

• What would it cost you to speak truth about problems you've witnessed?

• When the children in your life tell your story, what will they say you protected?

Discussion prompt:

Think about a time you saw a system fail someone vulnerable. What kept you from speaking up? What would need to change for you to act differently next time?

. . .

Part II: How Good Intentions Become Weapons

Chapters 3–4: When Faith and Authority Corrupt

Governor Holt's Grief

Personal tragedy (his daughter's murder) becomes justification for systematic elimination. His precise biblical citations reveal how scripture can be weaponized into policy.

Morrison's Blessing

A prison guard who found faith blesses weapons like communion. His arc reveals how religious language can sanctify violence when institutional power corrupts personal belief.

For reflection:

• How does personal pain sometimes make us support policies that hurt others?

• When have you seen religious or moral language used to justify harm?

• What institutions in your life use "good intentions" to avoid accountability?

Challenge:

Think about a policy you support. Who does it help? Who does it harm? What would the people it harms say about your good intentions?

Part III: Children Teaching Adults How to Love

Chapters 5–6: Lessons in Impossible Love

Maria's Sanctuary

A teenager builds family across racial and ideological lines, transforming Spanish lessons into a secret communication system. Her language becomes both bridge and weapon—creating connection while coordinating resistance. *Somos familia* becomes the signal for collective refusal.

DeShawn's Miracle

A diabetic young man shares insulin with a man whose ideology demands DeShawn's death. Through imperfect division, both survive—proving the mathematics of mercy multiply what fear divides.

For reflection:

• How do children in your life teach you about forgiveness and inclusion?

• When have you been surprised by kindness across lines of difference?

• What would change if your community practiced abundance instead of scarcity?

Practice:

Watch how children handle conflict this week. What do they choose that adults have forgotten how to do?

Part IV: The Price of Professional Distance

Chapters 7–8: When Careers Become Complicity

Dr. Volkova's Breaking Point

A scholar provides legitimacy for atrocity until she recognizes Mateo Rivera—a child who drew her butterflies at the free clinic—as Subject 84. When the abstract becomes personal, she risks her career to tell the truth.

Mama E's Silent Night

One woman alone with 222 names at 3:17 a.m., proving that witness-bearing sometimes means holding silence before speaking truth.

For reflection:

• How does your work contribute to systems that help or harm vulnerable people?

• When has professional obligation conflicted with personal conscience?

• What would make the abstract personal enough for you to act?

Part V: Justice or Just Performance?

Chapter 9: When Democracy Protects Itself

The federal trial convicts a man—but not the system. It highlights the illusion of progress without structural change.

For reflection:

• When have you seen "justice" that felt like performance?

• What problems are blamed on individuals instead of systems in your community?

• What scandals led to real change—and which didn't?

Part VI: How Memory Becomes Movement

Chapters 10–12: The Long Arc of Change

Mama E's Legacy

Teaches her granddaughter to carry the ledger forward, proving memory multiplies through generations.

Desmond's Evolution

From documenting death to disrupting elimination—the recorder becomes a tool for saving lives, not just counting the lost.

The Communion of Names

Across America, the work continues: diabetes clinics that never turn anyone away, schools teaching Spanish as resistance, federal laws protecting witnesses instead of eliminating them.

For reflection:

• How do you want to be remembered by the children in your life?

• What stories shaped your sense of right and wrong?

• How do you teach memory without trauma?

Legacy question:

What institutions in your life would miss you if you stopped participating? What would you want to change before you're gone?

Character Studies: Six Ways to Respond to Injustice

• **Desmond: The Investigator**

Tool: Recorder

Lesson: Some truths are worth dying for.

• **Mama E: The Witness-Bearer**

Tool: Ledger

Lesson: Memory is movement.

• **Dr. Volkova: The Recovering Accomplice**

Tool: Ethics education

Lesson: You can defect from systems that made you—but only when the abstract becomes personal.

• **Morrison: The Confessor**

Tool: Bible

Lesson: Faith means owning your part.

• **Maria: The Teacher**

Tool: Language as tactical resistance

Lesson: Education is revolution. (*Hermana* = stay close; *Abuela* = guards coming)

• **DeShawn: The Healer**

Tool: Insulin (shared imperfectly so both survive)

Lesson: Love multiplies what fear divides.

Themes That Challenge Everything

How Systems Turn Children into Statistics

Action step: Learn one name from a system you've ignored.

The Difference Between Memorial and Justice

Challenge: Identify what in your life honors harm instead of preventing it.

When Faith Becomes Weapon

Practice: Notice when sacred language is used to excuse cruelty.

The Mathematics of Mercy vs. the Mathematics of Murder

Reflection: Where in your life do you practice scarcity? Where could abundance change everything?

Understanding How Harm Spreads

• Follow the money behind incarceration

• Track who profits from policy

• Research your local universities' justice funding

What You Can Actually Do

In Your Household

• Teach conflict resolution through compassion

• Practice abundance with resources

• Model how to make amends

• Share stories of moral courage

In Your Community

• Support people with lived experience

• Volunteer where outcomes—not awareness—matter

• Create spaces where enemies can become family

• Challenge systems, not just people

In Your Civic Life

• Research candidates' justice records

• Testify at local hearings

• Document what you witness

• Join coalitions working on structural change

In Your Legacy

• Support youth-led organizing

• Teach children to write names like prayers

• Fund diabetes clinics and restorative schools

• Write your own ledger

Write Your Own Ledger
Who do you refuse to forget?

• The teacher who saw potential

• The child who taught you courage

• The "troublemaker" who made you think differently

• The stranger who shared when they didn't have enough

Start your ledger. Add to it. Share it.

Because naming the forgotten is the first step toward justice.

Because memory becomes movement when we refuse to let truth stay buried.

Because someone taught an eight-year-old that writing names right means writing them like they're smiling.

· · ·

The Final Word

Names Like Prayers proves that ordinary people can choose extraordinary courage.

That love survives in systems designed to eliminate it.

That children already know what justice looks like—we just stopped listening.

That the mathematics of mercy always balance when we stop subtracting people from the equation.

Write the names.

Speak the names.

Become the prayer.

Only then.

Always then.

Forever then.

Most of all then.

Somos familia.

ABOUT THE AUTHOR

Gene Scott grew up on a tenant farm in western Illinois, where stories around the kitchen table mixed magical realism with the gritty realities of hog farming, abandoned strip mines, and hot nuclear waste dumps.

After four decades in East Tennessee, he remains captivated by the audacity of nature —and its quiet power to heal what's broken, both physically and spiritually.

A prison ministry, and years of letters exchanged with inmates rediscovering themselves through Christian service and creative writing, helped inspire this novel.